W9-BEF-653

Adapted by RON FONTES and JUSTINE KORMAN
Based on the screenplay by JOHN HUGHES

TWENTIETH CENTURY FOX PRESENTS A JOHN HUGHES PRODUCTION BABY'S DAY OUT JOE MANTEGNA LARA FLYNN BOYLE JOEY PANTOLIANO
FILM EDITOR DAVID RAWLINS PRODUCTION DESIGNER DOUG KRANER DIRECTOR OF PHOTOGRAPHY THOMAS E. ACKERMAN EXECUTIVE PRODUCER WILLIAM RYAN CO-PRODUCER WILLIAM S. BEASLEY
WRITTEN BY JOHN HUGHES PRODUCED BY JOHN HUGHES AND RICHARD VANE DIRECTED BY PATRICK READ JOHNSON

Troll Associates

Once upon a time there was a beautiful baby named Bennington Austin Cotwell IV. But everyone called him Baby Bink. Bink lived in a big mansion with his mother, Laraine, his father, Bing, and his nanny, Gilbertine.

Every day Baby Bink wanted Gilbertine to read him the same storybook. It was called *Baby's Day Out*. The book was about a toddler named Baby Boo and his adventures in the big city.

"Couldn't we read another book?" Gilbertine asked. She was tired of reading about Baby Boo going to the zoo, and the department store, and the construction site, and . . .

Baby Bink shook his head and cried, "Boo-boo! Boo-boo!" That's what he called his favorite book.

While Gilbertine was reading to Baby Bink, his mother, Laraine, told her husband, "I've hired Downtown Baby Photographers to photograph the baby today. Their pictures always get published in the newspaper. And our friends are saying Baby Bink's unknown to society!"

Bing nodded. "It's time they opened their newspapers and saw the prettiest baby in this city."

Later that morning, the Downtown Baby Photographers' van pulled up in front of the Cotwell mansion. The three men who got out were dressed like photographers. But they were really crooks!

Eddie, Norby, and Veeko had tied up the real photographer and stolen his van.

Laraine was so excited about getting Baby Bink's picture published in the paper, she didn't notice how oddly the photographers acted.

"May I have some time alone with the child?" Eddie asked. "I need to study his marvelous little features."

Gilbertine handed him Baby Bink's book. "If he gets cranky, read him his book."

"Boo-boo!" Baby Bink cooed.

While Bink's mother and nanny were in the other room, Eddie took Baby Bink away from the mansion. The three crooks got into the van and drove away. Baby Bink was going on an adventure!

Everyone was extremely upset when they discovered that Baby Bink was gone.

Eddie, Norby, and Veeko took Baby Bink to their apartment in the big city. They didn't know much about kids.

"Any suggestions on how to get the junior human to sleep?" Norby asked.

"Read him his storybook — if you can," Eddie said.

So Norby read all about Baby Boo's trip to the big department store and the zoo and . . . Soon the crook was fast asleep.

But *Baby Bink* wasn't sleepy. He saw pigeons outside the window. They looked just like the birds in his "boo-boo." Baby Bink followed the pigeons onto the roof. He crawled past the big clock billboard. Then he crawled across a board to another roof. It was fun!

9

Eddie was furious when he realized Baby Bink was gone. "That little spit-up machine is my retirement money!" Eddie tried to jump from the roof to the next building. But he fell down and went BOOM!

The next thing the crooks knew, Baby Bink was waving to them from a big bus. It looked just like the bus in his "boo-boo"!

When the bus stopped, Norby asked, "Is there a baby on this bus?"

The driver shook his head. "I haven't picked up anyone traveling with a baby today."

"He was by himself," Norby said.

The driver thought that was very strange, so he called his boss to report a missing baby. But Bink wasn't missing. He was hiding in a big woman's basket.

The big woman carried the basket off the bus. Veeko saw Baby Bink peeking out of the basket. Peek-a-boo!

When the crooks tried to take the woman's basket, she hit them very hard. BAM! BAM! BAM!

Then Baby Bink crawled into a big department store, just like the one in his "boo-boo." It was fun!

On his way out of the store, Baby Bink crawled past a TV reporter. Baby Bink was on the news! Eddie, Norby, and Veeko saw the news on TV. They raced to the department store.

13

By the time the crooks reached the store, Baby Bink was in a bright yellow taxi cab —- just like the one in his "boo-boo."

The crooks' van chased the bright yellow cab through the big city.

When the cab stopped, the crooks opened the door. But Baby Bink was not inside. He was crawling to the city zoo, just like the zoo in his "boo-boo"!

"Eddie!" Norby shrieked. He pointed to Baby Bink, who was crawling across the busy street.

The cab driver saw Baby Bink crawling through traffic too. He thought that was so strange, he called his boss.

Eddie, Norby, and Veeko followed Baby Bink to the ape house in the zoo. Baby Bink liked the big gorilla inside. And the gorilla liked Baby Bink!

But the gorilla *didn't* like Eddie, Norby, and Veeko — especially when they tried to take his little friend away. The gorilla's fist went BOP! BOP! BOP! The crooks didn't feel very well.

After lunch, Baby Bink said good-bye to his gorilla friend and went for a crawl through the park. From their van, the crooks saw Baby Bink crawl through a park tunnel.

One of the crooks grabbed Bink. "This just ain't your lucky day, short-pants!" the crook sneered.

But it wasn't the crooks' lucky day, either. Just then, the police noticed the van, which didn't belong parked in the park.

"Do you know anything about this vehicle?" they asked the crooks.

Eddie sat on a park bench and hid Baby Bink on his lap. "Yes sir," he said, trying not to sound scared. "That's our van."

While the police officers asked about the van, Bink crawled off into the woods.

Baby Bink crawled until he saw a construction site, just like the one in his "boo-boo." Bink saw some donuts on a big metal girder. He crawled onto the girder and ate a delicious donut.

A crane lifted the girder high in the air. What a fun ride! Baby Bink saw the whole city stretched out beneath him. It was even prettier than the city in his "boo-boo"!

The crooks spotted Baby Bink at the construction site. They followed him inside. But they did not have a fun ride.

In fact, every time Eddie, Norby, and Veeko tried to grab Bink, something bad happened to them.

Then a loud whistle blew. It was 5 o'clock — time for the construction workers to go home. Baby Bink followed them out of the site.

One worker said, "I just saw a baby crawl out of the site!"

He thought it was so strange, he called the police.

"Help!" Eddie called. "Norby! Veeko!"

Baby Bink was gone again. Eddie was tired and bruised and stuck in midair, hanging from a crane. "That's it! I'm throwing in the towel. The caper's over."

Eddie went home and decided he would never have anything to do with babies again. He was going to go back to robbing banks.

Meanwhile, back at the Cotwell mansion, an FBI agent said, "This morning we received word of a man looking for a lost baby on a bus. Then someone reported a baby alone in a department store. This afternoon, a baby was seen in the park and the zoo, and finally at —"

Gilbertine suddenly cried, "A building under construction! He's doing everything in the book. I know where he is!"

Soon Bing, Laraine, and Gilbertine were standing in the lobby of the Old Soldier's Home, just like the one Baby Boo visited on his way home from the big city. They saw Baby Bink clapping his hands while the old soldiers sang.

"Baby!" Laraine cried. Then she scooped Bink up in her arms for a tight hug.

Laraine never wanted to let go of Baby Bink again. As their limousine drove through the city toward home, Bing patted Bink's head. "You had quite an adventure today!"

Suddenly, Baby Bink pointed and cried, "Boo-boo! Boo-boo!" He saw the building with the big clock on top.

"Boo-boo?" Bing asked.

"That's what he calls the book he lost today," Gilbertine explained.

"We'll buy you another one," Laraine promised.

But Baby Bink kept pointing and crying. "Boo-boo!"

Laraine finally understood. "He means his 'boo-boo' is back there. That's where he's been!"

The limousine raced toward the building with the big clock on top. Sirens wailed as police cars zoomed there too.

A police officer called up to the crooks' apartment. "You're surrounded. Throw down the 'boo-boo' and put your hands over your heads."

Eddie threw the storybook out the window. It opened to the last page, which showed Baby Boo at home with his mother and father. Then the police took away the crooks.

That night, Baby Bink lay snug and safe in his crib after his busy day in the big city. He was already looking forward to his next adventure!